First published in Great Britain in 1985 by
Octopus Books Limited

This edition published in 1988 by
Treasure Press
59 Grosvenor Street
London W1

ISBN 1 85051 262 0

Printed in Hong Kong

# JACK
## —AND THE—
# BEANSTALK

## Designed and illustrated
## —by—
# GERDA MULLER

TREASURE PRESS

Jack lived with his mother in a broken-down cottage which was surrounded by a small garden in which a few vegetables grew. His father had died when Jack was still a little child. The years had gone by. Jack was now a strong twelve-year-old boy, able to run fast, climb trees and do jobs to help his mother. His mother had to work hard to get enough money for them to live on.

While she was sewing and doing embroidery for her customers, Jack dug the garden, sowed the radishes, looked after the tomatoes, and climbed the apple tree to pick the fruit. It was Jack, too, who was responsible for looking after their great treasure, Clover, the brown and white cow. Thanks to Clover they had plenty of milk and butter. Each day Jack led her out to the meadow.

One winter the weather was exceptionally cold. The wood supply began to run out and the cost of bread rose steeply. Orders for sewing and embroidery grew fewer and fewer, and the pitiful savings of the widow began to melt away like snow in the sun. Clover had grown old. She yielded less and less milk. And, to crown their misery, hard frosts in early spring killed off their small crop of vegetables.

'My boy,' his mother said to Jack one day, 'we have only a few pennies left to buy a little bread, and that won't keep us alive for long. Clover is costing us money; we shall have to get rid of her. Tomorrow you must take her to market to be sold.'

'Sell Clover!' exclaimed Jack. 'What will become of us?'

'What else can we do if we don't want to die of hunger?' answered his mother. 'I know how sad you will be, but we don't have any choice. You must get a good price for her, and then we can survive until the fine weather comes again.'

Jack had a generous heart and loved his mother tenderly, but he was apt to be giddy and impulsive, and to believe whatever he was told. So his mother was uneasy about giving him this job, but she could not go to the market herself. She had an order for a christening bonnet which had to be finished that week.

Early the next day Jack passed a rope round Clover's neck and set off for the nearby town, feeling very sad.

After walking for a good hour, he came to a crossroads where he met a funny little man. This man had long white hair and he wore a beard which hung down to his middle. He had on such strange clothes that Jack felt like laughing when he looked at him. But he kept a straight face, thinking that it would be bad manners to laugh, and taking off his cap he politely greeted the stranger.

'Good day,' said the man in a sour voice. 'Where are you going with that cow?'

'Alas!' replied Jack, 'I am taking her to market, and that makes me very sad.'

The man questioned Jack and learned how poor he and his mother had become.

'Well then, Jack, you seem to be a fine boy,' he said. 'I should like to make you an offer.' And, taking a little leather purse from under his jacket, he exclaimed:

'I have here something that will make your mother and you happy for the rest of your days. I will give it to you if you let me have the cow in exchange.'

While he was speaking, he opened the purse and from it he took a handful of coloured seeds that looked like beans.

'You are making fun of me,' cried Jack. 'Beans in exchange for a cow!'

'These are not ordinary beans,' said the old man. 'They have a magic property. If you plant them they will bring you great riches.'

Jack said to himself that his mother would be happy with such an exchange. Without further thought he gave Clover a final pat, and put the beans in his pocket. Then he went back home whistling.

'Back already!' said his mother, uneasy at seeing him return so soon. 'At least you have sold Clover profitably! How much did you get for her?'

'I didn't get any money, mother dear,' answered Jack, 'but something much more valuable than that. Look!' And he took the handful of beans from his pocket. 'These are magic beans,' he said proudly. 'Thanks to them we shall be rich.'

When she saw the beans Jack's mother was so disappointed and unhappy that she snatched them up and threw them on the ground, saying:

'Jack, are you crazy? How did you come to exchange our cow for these miserable beans? Go to bed at once! There is nothing to eat for supper.'

Crestfallen, Jack climbed upstairs to bed with an empty stomach. The next day he woke early. But instead of the rays of the sun coming as usual to tickle the end of his nose, this morning the room was plunged in gloom. Jack saw that a thick curtain of leaves had formed itself in front of the window.

He got up, dressed himself quickly and crept down silently to the garden. There a surprise awaited him. By the side of the house, where the beans had fallen, a gigantic bean plant had grown up during the night. It was so big that its branches were lost in the clouds, and strain his eyes as he might, Jack could not see where they ended.

Without giving himself time to think, he sprang up the stalk of the bean plant, which was as thick as the trunk of a tree.

Jack climbed and climbed for a long time. Looking down towards the earth he made out, far, far below, his home, now grown tiny. He went on climbing and, on emerging from some thick clouds, he soon arrived in a strange country.

A vast heath stretched out before him. Here and there big rocks, making dark shadows, were strewn across the dry grass. The light was dazzling and the heat intense. Jack felt sorry he had not brought something to drink with him.

Worn out by the climb, Jack sat down in the shade of one of the rocks to recover his breath. Suddenly, he looked up and saw the old man who had given him the beans the day before.

'Oh!' exclaimed Jack, 'I'm sorry that I listened to you! Now we are still poorer than we were before, since we no longer even have our cow.'

'Don't be sad,' the old man said, 'and listen closely to what I tell you. Not far from here there lives a giant who once stole three treasures from me. I give them to you gladly because you are a good boy and you deserve them.'

'But,' he went on, 'you will have to seize them yourself. There I cannot help you. You will have to run great risks and be brave and daring in order to succeed. The giant of whom I spoke lives not far from here. Visit him. You will certainly find a way of taking back what he has stolen from me. But be careful. He is a fierce ogre.'

With these words the old man disappeared as suddenly as he had come.

Jack was a little frightened by this. However, the thought of how he might help his mother gave him courage and he strode off in the direction the old man had indicated.

The way was long and the heat intense, but Jack walked on without taking a rest. He finally reached a great building which seemed to be the giant's house. With a beating heart he knocked at the door.

An extremely tall woman opened it.

'Have pity on me,' Jack said to her. 'I am hungry. I am half dead with thirst. Let me come in and give me something to eat and drink.'

'Alas, poor boy,' she answered, 'if I allow you to come in here you will not come out again alive. My master will soon be back. He is a fierce ogre. If he sees you, he will eat you up. So take my advice, continue on your way and try somewhere else.'

'I don't have the strength to go on,' said Jack. He was really afraid, but he hid his fear. 'When your master returns I shall hide and he won't see me.'

Pitying him, the woman allowed him to go in and gave him a plate of soup and a glass of milk. Scarcely had Jack finished his meal than a terrible noise was heard. It was the giant coming home again. The woman hurriedly thrust Jack into a food-cupboard that was already full of hams and sides of beef, closed the door, and went to welcome her master.

'Fee, fi, fo, fum,' said the giant, 'I smell the blood of an Englishman! Some delicacy is hidden and I mean to make my dinner of it.'

As he was searching everywhere, he was interrupted by his servant, who said:

'That will be the young calf which I have prepared for you. Here it is. Sit down at the table.'

Ravenously hungry, the giant sat down and devoured a whole calf, several haunches of mutton and a roast duck, all of which his servant pressed him to eat up.

Jack was spying through a crack in the food-cupboard and he saw everything. When the giant had finished his meal he ordered his servant to take off his boots.

'Bring me my sacks of gold,' he said, 'so that I can play with them a little.'

His servant brought him three sacks filled with gold coins. Then she left the room, casting an uneasy glance at the food-cupboard in which Jack was shut up.

The giant entertained himself for some time by emptying the sacks and filling them up again. Suddenly, overcome by fatigue – and after such a large meal there was nothing surprising about that – he lay down on his bed and fell into a deep sleep.

Jack crept on tiptoe out of the food-cupboard and went up to the table. The giant's snores now shook the whole house. Jack cautiously helped himself to one of the sacks and left the room. He succeeded in getting out of the house without meeting anyone and hurried away as fast as the heavy weight of the sack would let him.

Jack walked with difficulty, bent over under the heavy load, and big drops of sweat fell from his forehead. His pace slowed down, but he never stopped. He thought of his mother's joy when she saw the sack and that gave him strength.

Reaching the beanstalk, he climbed right down it. This was by no means easy and it took a long time before he reached the ground.

'Mother! Mother!' he called out. 'Quickly come and see!'

His mother ran up. She had been worried all the morning, wondering what had become of Jack. She was overjoyed to see him again. And just imagine her joy when he showed her what was in the sack!

'Thanks to the kindness of the old man and to your courage, Jack dear, we shall have enough money to live on for a long time!' said she, hugging her son.

So Jack and his mother lived very comfortably for nearly a year. With the giant's money they were able to buy a young cow and a few rabbits. Jack sowed some radishes, planted some lettuces, and trimmed the apple tree. The garden flourished.

But, as ill-luck would have it, a winter even more severe than the last one brought new trials to these poor people. Jack and his mother could no longer save. They had to part with all they possessed, and once more they found themselves penniless.

'Don't worry, mother,' said Jack. 'I will return to the giant's house and I shall certainly find some other treasure that I can bring home to help us.'

His mother was uneasy at seeing her son depart, but she could not stop him. Jack climbed up the beanstalk, passed through the clouds, and arrived at the country of the giant. He then put on a disguise which he had brought with him and which made him look like a poor, small girl. Then he knocked at the door of the big building. As before, it was opened by the woman.

'Pity me,' said Jack, disguising his voice. 'I am hungry. I am half-dead from thirst. Let me come in and give me something to eat and drink.'

'Alas, my poor little girl,' replied the woman, who had not recognised Jack. 'If I let you come in here, you will not come out again alive. My master will soon be back. He is a fierce ogre.'

'He has become worse than ever since a small boy, whom I had helped, stole one of his sacks of gold coins. If he sees you he will eat you up. So take my advice, continue on your way and try somewhere else.'

But Jack did not listen.

'I don't have the strength to go on,' he said. 'When your master returns I shall hide and he won't see me.'

The woman, who was very soft-hearted, allowed him to go in and gave him a plate of soup and a glass of milk. Hardly had Jack finished his meal than a terrible noise was heard. It was the giant coming home again. The woman, beside herself, thrust Jack into a big tub in which meat was salted and put the lid back on it. Just in time!

'Fee, fi, fo, fum. I smell the blood of an Englishman!' exclaimed the giant as soon as he was seated. 'That smells like fresh meat. Such a delicacy won't escape me!'

He searched everywhere, opening the cupboard doors, looking inside the food-cupboard and peering into the oven. He was approaching the tub when the woman brought him a savoury stew-pot in which a side of beef was simmering.

Ravenous, the giant sat down at the table and started his meal. He swallowed the side of beef, then he ate a whole sheep, and finally a gigantic turkey, which he consumed in a few bites. But between each dish he abused the woman, and altogether he seemed to be in a thoroughly bad mood. Finally, after a long drink of wine, he became a little calmer.

'Take off my boots,' he said to the servant, 'and bring me my hen so that I can entertain myself. But,' he added in a terrifying voice, 'keep a sharp look-out and be sure no one comes in, otherwise I shall beat you!'

The poor woman took off her master's boots, and then she brought him a fine white hen which she placed on the table, meanwhile casting frightened glances in the direction of the tub.

Jack had seen everything through a chink in the wood, and he scarcely dared breathe, so afraid was he of being caught.

The giant looked at the hen and then, in a voice like thunder, he cried: 'Hen, lay!'

Immediately the white hen laid a beautiful golden egg.

Each time the giant gave the order, she laid a golden egg. Suddenly the giant felt tired. His eyes closed and his head flopped over onto the table. He slept.

As soon as his snores became regular, Jack quietly raised the lid and crept out of the tub.He removed his disguise,went up to the table, grabbed the hen and climbed out of the window.
At that moment the hen started to cackle and the giant woke up.

Jack ran as hard as he could to the beanstalk, holding on to the hen. But the giant caught up with him in a few paces. He was just about to grab Jack when he tripped on a rock and fell full-length on the ground.

Jack lost no time in creeping through the bean leaves and sliding down the whole length of the stalk. By the time the giant had got up Jack had disappeared and as he could see him nowhere, he gave up the chase. Jack was saved.

When he reached home his mother, who had been very worried about him, was happy indeed to see him safe and sound.

The hen was given a pretty basket and was fed with the finest grain that money could buy. Each morning she laid a golden egg, so Jack and his mother were freed from want.

The house was repaired, the roof covered in fresh thatch, the beams repainted, the walls lime-washed. Every room was cheerfully papered.

Everyone who knocked at the door was made welcome and no one left empty-handed.

A year went by in this state of happiness. But one day Jack's mother fell sick. In spite of the care with which Jack looked after her, she grew steadily worse.

Feeling hopeless, Jack no longer knew what to do. Finally, he decided to return to the country of the giant. Perhaps he would be able to bring back from it some medicine that would make his mother well again.

'Go,' she told him. 'But do not be away too long. I have not strength enough to live alone.'

'Don't worry, mother,' Jack replied. 'Be brave and wait for me to come back. I shall return with something to cure you.'

He climbed up the beanstalk, passed through the clouds and arrived at the country of the giant. Here it was always hot, the light was always dazzling, but nothing could stop Jack. He had dressed himself up in a new disguise that made him look like a beggar, and he knocked at the door of the big building. As before, it was opened by the woman.

'Have pity on me,' said Jack, disguising his voice. 'I am hungry, I am half dead with thirst. Let me come in and give me something to eat and drink.'

'Alas, my poor child,' answered the woman. 'If I allow you to come in here you will not come out alive. My master will soon be back. He is a fierce ogre. He has become very suspicious since his gold coins and his white hen were stolen. If he sees you, he will eat you up. So take my advice, continue on your way and try somewhere else.'

But Jack was so insistent that the woman finally gave in to him. She allowed him to go in and she gave him a plate of soup and a glass of milk. Scarcely had he finished his meal than a terrible noise was heard. It was the giant coming home again. He grunted and he grumbled and altogether he seemed to be furious.

Hardly had he crossed the threshold than he exclaimed:

'Fee, fi, fo, fum. I smell the blood of an Englishman! Ho there, woman! You have allowed someone to come in. I'll beat you as flat as a pancake, and break all your bones!'

The poor servant tremblingly replied that she had seen no one, and begged her master to eat the meat which she was roasting for him. So saying, she carried in one of the haunches of pork which was turning on a spit in front of the fire.

The giant sat down and ate first one, then a second, then a third of these haunches.

Then he got up and began to poke about in every corner of the room.

'Someone is here, I can tell,' he said, rolling his eyes ferociously. 'And if he falls into my hands I shall eat him up in a single mouthful!'

The woman never stopped filling up his plate, but no sooner had he emptied it than he got up again and continued his search. Jack had barely had time to slide under the bed, and he shook with fear every time the giant drew near him.

Meanwhile the giant had opened all the cupboards, and the food-cupboard, and he had taken the lids off the tub and the bread bin. He was growing really impatient when the woman said to him:

'You have just eaten a whole pig and nearly half an ox. Isn't that enough for you? I have a dozen chickens ready and done to a turn. Would you like them?'

'Let me have them,' said the giant. 'I am still ravenous.'

And he picked up the chickens and ate them one after another, without bothering to separate the meat from the bones. Hardly had he finished off the whole dozen of them than the woman brought him a great pitcher of wine. He tossed it off in a single gulp and then, in a voice of thunder, he told her to take off his boots and bring him his magic harp.

The woman took off the giant's boots and put a little harp, made out of gilded wood, on the table.

'Harp, play!' ordered the giant, and the harp began to play. Marvellous music, sweet and lovely, filled the room. As soon as he heard the first notes Jack had only one thought: to get hold of the harp. Such music, he felt sure, could not fail to restore his mother's health. Whatever it cost he must have the harp.

The giant was now in a sunny good humour. He stretched out his legs in front of the fire and rocked himself to and fro in time with the music. It was not long before he fell asleep. Soon his snores were making the house shake.

Jack crept out from underneath the bed, went up to the table and grabbed the harp. He passed its strap over his shoulder and was just getting ready to jump over the window ledge when the harp, which was a magic one, cried out:

'Help, master, help!'

Instantly the giant woke up. Jack wasted no time; he jumped out of the room and started to run away. He ran and he ran, faster than he had ever run before. His disguise, which he had not had time to remove, got in his way and the giant was just behind him.

Every now and then the giant stopped to rub his feet, which he had bruised on the rocks, and this slowed him up. But for every single pace the giant took, Jack had to take ten, and the chase could not last long. Jack, never turning round, was soon out of breath. He knew that if he could reach the beanstalk before the giant caught him, he would be saved. But could he get there in time?

At last, just as he felt the giant breathing down his neck, Jack was able to plunge in amongst the leaves and as fast as he could, to clamber down the whole length of the beanstalk.

Surprised, the giant hesitated for a moment, then he too climbed downwards.

The branches tore his clothes and he was so big that he became entangled in the leaves.

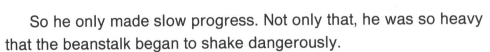

So he only made slow progress. Not only that, he was so heavy that the beanstalk began to shake dangerously.

Jack had now got to the bottom. What a surprise! The old man to whom he owed all his luck and happiness was waiting for him. Silently, he offered Jack an axe which Jack at once grasped.

The beanstalk was thick and it needed several blows of the axe to make an impression on it. The weight of the giant did the rest. Suddenly a crack was heard and the beanstalk fell. It was so big that its top crashed into the sea several miles away. With it fell the giant and nothing more was ever heard of him.

Without waiting to see what had happened, Jack looked everywhere for the old man to thank him. He had vanished. Then Jack ran to his mother's bedroom and placed the harp on the table. The poor woman, pale and exhausted, was breathing faintly and seemed to be asleep.

'Harp, play!' said Jack.

The harp, freed from the spell which bound it to the giant, obeyed its new master and began to play.

In a few moments the colour returned to the sick woman's cheeks, her eyelids trembled, and she woke up and smiled. The music which filled the room was so lovely that Jack's mother felt better. She asked for something to eat and drink. And the happiness of seeing her son again completed the cure.

Jack and his mother lived happily ever afterwards, doing good to all around them. Anyone who was poor, or sad, or sick could knock on their door and it was sure to be opened wide in welcome. The visitor would be seated in a comfortable armchair and offered a delicious meal and a reviving drink, while the magic harp played its wonderful music. Little by little his cares and worries would disappear and he would start to feel better. Soon he would be able to go on his way again, head held high.

And, each year, Jack grew a little bean plant in his garden in memory of the giant beanstalk which brought him all his good fortune.